MW00617271

A Permanent Image

Samuel D. Hunter

A SAMUEL FRENCH ACTING EDITION

SAMUEL FRENCH

FOUNDED 1830

SAMUELFRENCH.COM
SAMUELFRENCH-LONDON.CO.UK

FOR PRODUCTION ENQUIRIES

UNITED STATES AND CANADA
Info@SamuelFrench.com
1-866-598-8449

UNITED KINGDOM AND EUROPE
Plays@SamuelFrench-London.co.uk
020-7255-4302

Each title is subject to availability from Samuel French, depending upon
country of performance. Please be aware that *A PERMANENT IMAGE*
may not be licensed by Samuel French in your territory. Professional
and amateur producers should contact the nearest Samuel French
office or licensing partner to verify availability.

MUSIC USE NOTE

Licensees are solely responsible for obtaining formal written permission from copyright owners to use copyrighted music in the performance of this play and are strongly cautioned to do so. If no such permission is obtained by the licensee, then the licensee must use only original music that the licensee owns and controls. Licensees are solely responsible and liable for all music clearances and shall indemnify the copyright owners of the play(s) and their licensing agent, Samuel French, against any costs, expenses, losses and liabilities arising from the use of music by licensees. Please contact the appropriate music licensing authority in your territory for the rights to any incidental music.

IMPORTANT BILLING AND CREDIT REQUIREMENTS

If you have obtained performance rights to this title, please refer to your licensing agreement for important billing and credit requirements.

A PERMANENT IMAGE was commissioned and first produced by Boise Contemporary Theater, in Boise, Idaho on November 22, 2011. The performance was directed by Kip Fagan, with sets by Etta Lilienthal, costumes by Jessica Pabst, lights by Raquel Davis, sound by Jay Spriggs, videos by Andy Lawless, props by Bernadine Cockey, and dramaturgy by John M. Baker. The Production Stage Manager was Kristy J. Martin. The cast was as follows:

CAROL . . . . .Lynne McCollough
BO . . . . Matthew Cameron Clark
ALLY . . . . .Danielle Slavick
MARTIN. . . . . Arthur Glen Hughes

CHARACTERS

CAROL – Early-to-mid sixties, female.

BO – Carol's son; mid-to-late thirties, male.

ALLY – Carol's daughter; early-to-mid thirties, female.

MARTIN *(on video only)* – Carol's husband, Bo and Ally's father; early-to-mid sixties, male.

SETTING

The interior of a small, ranch-style house in Viola, a small town of about 700 people in northern Idaho. There is a well-worn couch, some withered plants, some shelves with pictures and trinkets on them, a TV with a wood frame, a dining table, and some sad looking Christmas decorations including a fake tree. Everything in the space – aside from the Christmas decorations and the screen of the television – has been crudely painted white. Every piece of furniture, framed picture, shelf, trinket, book, magazine, the floor, the walls. The effect should be that the Christmas decorations are the only bit of color on an otherwise completely white set.

TIME

The present.

AUTHOR'S NOTES

Dialogue written in italics is emphatic, slow, and deliberate; dialogue in ALL CAPS is impulsive, quick, explosive. Dialogue written in BOTH is a combination of the two.

A "/" indicates an overlap in dialogue.

ACT ONE

Home Video

(The TV flickers to life and we see a shot of **MARTIN** *on the living room couch. The living room appears as it did before it was painted white.)*

MARTIN. I'm not really sure how to do this. Carol wants me to do this.

CAROL. *(offscreen)* We *both* want you to / do this.

MARTIN. We both – we both want this, we both do.

> *(pause)*

Now you may think we're gonna apologize, or whatever. We're not gonna do that, that's pointless. Waste of tape.

> *(pause)*

I guess the universe is expanding? I don't understand it completely, but it's something about how we all started out from this little thing, the big bang or whatever, and now everything in the universe is just splaying out in all these directions, and some people actually think it's getting faster – it's actually been proven, it's all / getting –

CAROL. *(offscreen)* Martin would you just get / to the –

MARTIN. You gonna let me talk or not?

CAROL. *(offscreen)* I'm letting you talk! Just get to the point!

MARTIN. Anyway – a lot of people think that eventually it's all just gonna go in reverse, come crashing down. All of us, everything in the universe shoved back into this tight little ball. Eventually.

(pause)

MARTIN. I actually find that comforting. You need to know
that I – that *we* – find it comforting.

(The TV turns off and the lights rise on:)

Scene One

(**BO** *sits on the couch center stage, looking around the space.* **CAROL** *is busying herself with minutiae; arranging things, coming in and out of the kitchen, bringing* **BO** *snacks. A small stereo plays "Angels We Have Heard On High" in the background.*)

CAROL. – and she was a real pill about it, believe me. But I told her, if you're going to let that stupid dog roam around the whole town all day long, then I'm going to shoot it if I see it in my garden. It's just BB's anyway, not like it would –. And I wouldn't aim for its head. Just give it a little shock, that's it. It's not cruel. Do you want a beer?

(*no response*)

Bo?

(*pause*)

BO. Yeah okay.

(**CAROL** *exits to the kitchen, continuing to talk.*)

CAROL. So she brings me the vet bill for something like three hundred dollars, she said she had them X-ray the stupid dog and everything, and after all that there's just a few BB's inside of him, not in his organs or anything –

(**CAROL** *enters with two Budweisers, hands one to* **BO**, *opens one for herself.*)

– just right underneath the skin. So he's fine, and she wants three hundred dollars from me or something. She's such a dunce.

BO. You're having one?

CAROL. Yeah, I'm having one. What the hell is that supposed to mean?

BO. No, it's just.

CAROL. It's just a beer for God's sake, doesn't mean anything.

BO. I just didn't know you were drinking.

CAROL. I'm not drinking, it's *beer*.

BO. Mom.

CAROL. One beer, for God's sake.

BO. Mom.

CAROL. What?

>   *(Silence.* **BO** *stares at her.)*

BO. *Mom.*

CAROL. *WHAT I said?!*

BO. *Why the hell is everything painted white?!*

>   **(CAROL** *looks at him for a few moments. She's about to say something, then stops herself. She stands up, exits to the kitchen.)*

CAROL. *(from the kitchen)* I bought these stupid snack trays at Costco. They're sort of stupid, I have a lot of them.

>   **(CAROL** *re-enters with a small snack tray with some meat, cheese, and crackers on it. She sits on the couch with* **BO**.)

I bought them because I thought we might have people over after the funeral but I don't think I want to do that so let's just eat them.

BO. I'm not – I'm not hungry.

CAROL. Well there's a lot of them. You look thin anyway.

BO. Mom.

CAROL. God would you stop saying that?

BO. Did you – when did you do all this?

CAROL. Oh I don't know. Couple days ago.

BO. Right after Dad died?

CAROL. Oh I don't know.

BO. You *don't know?*

CAROL. *GAH* would you stop it? You're really at me today.

BO. Have you been drinking?

CAROL. Again with the drinking!

BO. How much have you been drinking these past few days?

CAROL. Oh dear Lord. Yesterday I had three beers. Day before, I don't remember, I think I had a glass of wine. Again with the drinking!

BO. That's all? Seriously?

CAROL. Bo please stop.

BO. Well what – ?! What do you expect me to do?!

CAROL. What?!

BO. THE HOUSE!

CAROL. IT'S MY HOME I CAN DO WHATEVER I WANT. I just needed a change, okay? And I didn't have the money to buy all new things so I just thought this was a good idea, and I still think it's a good idea and I would appreciate some support with this.

BO. Oh my God.

CAROL. Oh stop it. Have some food.

> (*pawing at the snack tray*)

What is this, salami? Ech. Have it.

> (**BO** *stands up, looking around.*)

BO. But I mean – the pictures? My God, is this a magazine? You painted over a magazine?

CAROL. I was out in the shed and there was all this white paint, I thought why not? Anyway, I'm bored by this conversation.

BO. Mom, do I need to call someone? Do I need to call the hospital or something?

CAROL. Bo, I haven't gone crazy. I know it seems that way but I really haven't. It's just

> (*pause*)

Were your flights okay?

> (*pause*)

BO. They were fine.

CAROL. I called you three days ago, I don't know why you had to wait until today to travel. Christmas Eve of all days, the airports must've been awful.

BO. I couldn't get out until today. It wasn't that bad.

CAROL. Did you go home first?

BO. No, I told you, I just flew straight here.

CAROL. You spend too much time traveling. It's not healthy, you should spend more time at home. Though New York isn't much better.

BO. You've never even been there.

CAROL. Of course I've never been there, I don't want to get *raped*.

BO. Oh my God.

CAROL. I don't know why you're spending your life to go to such God awful places.

BO. It's my job.

CAROL. Why can't you take pictures of normal things?

BO. No one wants pictures of normal things.

CAROL. That's ridiculous. What, am I going to put a framed picture of some corpse or whatever on my mantle? Take pictures of sunsets, cats, babies with spaghetti on their heads or whatever, I'll put that on a mantle.

BO. Uh huh.

CAROL. Anyway, Ally's coming tonight. Laura and Max are coming later for some reason, God knows why. When was the last time you saw her?

BO. I don't know. Few years.

CAROL. Funeral's tomorrow at five, at two we're doing the body watching thing.

BO. You mean the viewing?

CAROL. Whatever. I'm having him cremated.

BO. Dad always said he didn't want to be cremated.

CAROL. Oh he didn't know what he was saying. Did you bring clothes for the funeral?

BO. Yeah, I –

CAROL. We can go to the dress-for-less if you need to.

BO. No, I don't – . Okay, did you do this because you're – grieving? Are you trying to like, forget about Dad, or -

CAROL. You know just because you went to college doesn't mean you're a psychiatrist.

BO. It doesn't take a psychiatrist to know that this is fucking crazy!

CAROL. DON'T USE THAT WORD.

BO. It's just I'm not sure how to deal with this, Mom! This is obviously some cry for attention, or / some kind of –

CAROL. Oh thank you. Thank you, Doctor Freud.

BO. I don't know what to do with this!

CAROL. You don't have to do anything!

BO. Obviously I do!

CAROL. FINE THEN LOCK ME UP!

BO. Oh here we go.

CAROL. CALL THE AUTHORITIES! PADDY WAGON! CRAZY / WOMAN!

BO. Mom –

CAROL. MAN DIES AND HIS WIFE GOES INSANITY, THERE'S YOUR HEADLINE!

BO. WHAT ARE YOU TALKING ABOUT?!

CAROL. WHY ARE WE FIGHTING ALREADY?!

BO. WE'RE NOT FIGHTING!

CAROL. I JUST PAINTED EVERYTHING WHITE! I'M NOT CRAZY!

BO. FINE THEN!

CAROL. OKAY?

BO. OKAY!

CAROL. HAVE THE STUPID SNACK TRAY!

(Lights snap to black, then rise on:)

Scene Two

(That night. **BO** *is sitting on the couch watching the television next to a box marked "April – May 1992." His suitcase is open on the floor.)*

(There is a small projector set up, **BO** *plays an old Super 8 film, projecting it onto the wall. The shot is blurry and distorted, but it's clear that it's a shot of a small child sleeping in a bed. Nothing is moving in the picture.* **BO** *moves to the projector, stops the film.)*

(He takes the film out of the projector, puts it back in the box, starts rooting through it a bit.)

(ALLY *appears in the doorway, wearing jeans and a parka, and holding a duffel bag.* **BO** *doesn't notice her enter.)*

(ALLY *immediately notices the interior of the house has been completely painted white. She moves into the space slowly, setting down her duffel bag silently.* **BO***'s back is still turned to her. She continues to survey the space for a few more moments, moving closer to* **BO***. Finally she is right behind him.)*

(A brief silence, then:)

ALLY. WHAT THE FUCK HAPPENED TO THE HOUSE?!

*(***BO** *drops the box of tapes, terrified. He spins around.)*

BO. *SHHH!* Jesus Christ she finally went to bed!

ALLY. *What the hell happened here?!*

BO. You didn't know about this?

ALLY. No I didn't know about this!

BO. Why the hell did it take you so long to get here? You live three hours away and you show up the night before the funeral? I flew here from *Tel Aviv* and I got here before you.

ALLY. I had shit to do, Bo, I own a business, I can't just – …
What happened to the house?!

BO. I don't know, okay? It was like this when I came in here this afternoon. She said she just wanted to paint everything white, I don't know. She did it after Dad died.

ALLY. Is she drinking?

BO. Some, I don't know. She says not a lot but God knows.

> *(pause)*

Have you noticed anything weird about her? Has she been off in any way, does she – ?

ALLY. I don't know. She's always a little off.

BO. No, but I mean – the last time you were here, was anything – off?

> *(pause)*

ALLY. God, I don't remember.

BO. How long ago was it?

ALLY. Bo, I'm tired.

BO. *How long was it?*

> *(pause)*

ALLY. Like – a couple years ago? Who knows.

BO. A *couple years ago?*

ALLY. WHEN WAS THE LAST TIME YOU WERE HERE?

BO. I LIVE THREE THOUSAND MILES AWAY!

> *(catching himself)*

> *FUCK. SHHHH.*

ALLY. Bo, I have a life. I can't drive here every weekend / to –

BO. No one's asking you to come every weekend, / but –

ALLY. You think I *enjoy* coming back here for God's sake? Why are you blaming me?!

BO. I'm not – . Okay, okay, enough. We're done now, okay? We're done.

ALLY. Fine. Good.

(*pause*)

BO. Hi, Ally.

ALLY. Yeah, whatever. Hi Bo.

(*pause*)

Hi.

(*pause*)

BO. Am I gonna get to meet Max?

ALLY. I don't know. He's – hard to travel with.

BO. Sure. He's what six, seven months?

ALLY. Dammit Bo, he's two. He just turned two.

BO. Oh my God, I'm sorry. He's *two*?

ALLY. Yeah. I haven't seen you in four years, Laura had him two years ago.

(*pause*)

BO. Did you get the book I sent you for him?

ALLY. Yeah, we uh. We got that.

BO. What?

ALLY. It was weird, Bo, it's like a comic book about the Holocaust?

BO. It's a *graphic novel.*

ALLY. Well we started reading it to him, and it got pretty weird pretty fast.

BO. It's not – ! I didn't mean for you to give it to him *now*, I just thought he'd like it when he was older, I – . I don't know, I'm sorry. I don't know how to buy things for kids.

(*pause*)

ALLY. It's fine. It was nice.

BO. Anyway I hope I get to meet him.

(*pause*)

ALLY. He's great. He's smart, he loves people, he's – great.

BO. How's Laura?

ALLY. She's fine. Getting a little antsy staying at home all the time, but she's fine.

BO. Good, that's – that's really good.

(**ALLY** *moves to the couch, examines it, sits down.*)

ALLY. You think this could just be like the way she grieves? Like maybe she just needs to get it out of her system.

BO. I guess.

ALLY. Some people do weird shit when stuff like this happens. Laura's grandpa died two years ago and she went completely nuts for a week and a half. Barely recognized her. Took up *knitting*. She snapped out of it. You wanna smoke?

(**ALLY** *opens her duffel bag, pulls out a joint.*)

BO. Whoa.

ALLY. You think I could come back here *sober*?

BO. I figured you might have calmed down with that since having Max.

ALLY. You kidding? We live on thirty acres. We grow our own.

BO. *Jesus*, Ally, you could go to *prison* for / that –

ALLY. Calm down, the county sheriff is Max's godfather. It's just a few little plants in our greenhouse, anyway. You want some?

(*Pause.* **ALLY** *lights the joint.*)

BO. Yeah okay.

(**ALLY** *hands the joint to* **BO**. *He lights it, takes a drag. They pass it back and forth.*)

ALLY. Why are you looking through this stuff?

BO. I was just – . I don't know. We barely had a relationship after I left, I felt like I didn't even remember what he looked like. Did you know he was sick?

ALLY. He wasn't sick, it was just a heart attack.

(*pause*)

BO. How do you – … Are you – sad?

ALLY. Well, yeah, whatever. I guess.

BO. When Mom called me a few days ago, I didn't even answer, just let it go to voicemail. Later that night I actually listened to it, she just said, "Bo, Dad had a heart attack or something, he's gone. You should come home." I just – have no idea how to feel about all of this. After our childhoods, how the hell are we supposed to feel about this? Are we *supposed* to feel sad? Why should we?

ALLY. You don't need to psychoanalyze everything, you'll feel what you feel.

BO. Yeah. I don't know, I guess staring at those photos all day long doesn't help.

(**BO** *references an iPad sitting in his open duffel.*)

ALLY. Hey are your photos on that?

(**ALLY** *grabs the iPad.*)

BO. Um. Yeah, but – maybe you shouldn't –

(**ALLY** *turns on the iPad.*)

ALLY. C'mon, I never get to see your stuff.

(*She stops, horrified. Pause.*)

Oh.

BO. Just put it down.

ALLY. Oh my God.

(**ALLY** *looks for a second, then turns off the iPad, hands it back to* **BO**.)

I – I really wish I wouldn't have seen that.

BO. I told you not to look.

ALLY. You – took those? You were actually there, you saw that?

What magazine is gonna print that?

BO. Well, hopefully quite a few.

(*pause*)

You okay?

ALLY. Yeah, it's. It's just different now that I have a kid, that stuff gets to me.

BO. Yeah, I bet.

> (**CAROL** *enters from out of her bedroom in an old robe.*)

CAROL. You know it's almost midnight.

> (**ALLY** *turns around and faces* **CAROL**. *They look at one another for a moment.*)

ALLY. Hey, Mom.

> *(pause)*

You painted the house white. It's pretty fucking crazy.

CAROL. Hi Ally. Don't swear, it's man-ish.

> *(pause)*

It's good to see you.

> (**CAROL** *sees the box of video tapes, the camera hooked up to the TV.*)

What is that?

BO. Oh, I was just – I was looking through some of Dad's old videos –

CAROL. Where did you find that? What are you doing?

BO. Just – the laundry room closet, where they always are. What's the matter?

> (**CAROL** *grabs the box of tapes, goes to the projector and aggressively throws it into the box.*)

CAROL. You don't go pawing through people's things, for God's sake.

ALLY. Mom, it's not a big / deal –

CAROL. Oh it's not? You're going to tell me what a big deal is? Just leave things where they are! Don't go destroying my house!

ALLY. You already destroyed it!

BO. Mom, I'm – I'm / sorry –

CAROL. This is already going to be an unpleasant Christmas, so please just –

    (sees the joint)

Drugs! In my house!

    (CAROL grabs the joint.)

What are you both idiots? You're going to get me arrested! Running a drug house!

    (pause)

Dammit, it's nice to have you both back here. GO TO BED.

    (CAROL exits with the box while taking a drag of the joint.)

Scene Three

*(Much later that same night. **ALLY** is sitting at the dining table looking at the photographs on **BO**'s iPad. After a moment **CAROL** enters, **ALLY** shuts the iPad.)*

CAROL. It's almost three in the morning, what are you doing?

ALLY. Couldn't get to sleep.

CAROL. It's too cold, is that it?

ALLY. You painted my bed white.

(pause)

Why are you still up?

CAROL. Getting used to sleeping alone, I guess.

ALLY. That'd be hard.

CAROL. You kidding? It's great. I spent thirty-nine years sharing a full size bed with that man.

ALLY. So why aren't you sleeping?

CAROL. I don't know. It's cold.

*(**CAROL** goes to a liquor cabinet, takes out a bottle and two glasses.)*

You want some?

ALLY. You shouldn't be drinking that.

CAROL. And you shouldn't be smoking pot. I said do you want some?

(pause)

ALLY. Yeah, okay.

*(**CAROL** sits with **ALLY**, pours them both some drinks.)*

Mom, are you okay? You're not going crazy, are you?

CAROL. That's the last time I'm answering that question, you understand? I just wanted to do it, and I know it seems strange, but dammit let me grierve. Alright?

CAROL. *(re: the iPad)* What were you looking at?

ALLY. It's – nothing. Bo's pictures.

CAROL. Let me see.

ALLY. Mom you don't wanna see these.

CAROL. Oh just give it.

>   (**ALLY** *relents, turns on the iPad, shows it to*
>   **CAROL**. **CAROL** *looks at it.*)

This is Bo's? Bo took this?

ALLY. Yeah.

>   (**CAROL** *stops, gives the iPad back to* **ALLY**.)

CAROL. I don't understand how he came out of me. These interests of his. It's morbid. Why were you looking at that?

ALLY. I just – … I don't know, I just felt like looking at it.

CAROL. Well you shouldn't. Especially now that you have one of your own, it's gonna scramble your brain. When are Laura and Max coming? The funeral's tomorrow, I told you that, right?

ALLY. Um. I'm not – I'm not sure if they're going to make it, Mom.

CAROL. Not at all? That's crazy, it's your father's funeral! Plus I haven't seen Max since right after he was born.

ALLY. It's hard to travel with a two-year-old. You know. We'll see, maybe they can make it.

>   *(pause)*

Mom, do you – …

>   *(pause)*

CAROL. What?

ALLY. Were you with Dad when he died? You don't have to talk about it if you don't want to.

CAROL. It's okay, I can – … Yes, I was with him.

ALLY. So what happened? How did it happen?

CAROL. Well, he was sitting on the couch, I was sitting at the table right here. He was breathing, and then he wasn't. Then I called the police or whatever, they sent the coroner over and he balled him up in a white sheet and took him / to the –

ALLY. But I mean – what happened? What did he do?

CAROL. I told you. He was breathing, then he wasn't.

ALLY. But what did he *look* like?

CAROL. What the hell kind of question is that?

ALLY. Look, I – I don't really know how to feel about this, and I / just –

CAROL. Fine, what happened was a chorus of angels swooped in through the window and pulled him through the ceiling. It was all real magical, all rainbows and –

ALLY. OKAY MOM.

CAROL. Why do you want to know what it looked like?

ALLY. I don't know, I just – I don't know how to feel about it, okay? I haven't seen him in so long I feel like I can't even picture it, I have no idea what to feel.

CAROL. Listen to me. He was breathing, then he wasn't. He was my husband, then he wasn't. He was your Dad, then he wasn't. That's all. It's how I'll go, it's how you'll go.

(*pause*)

ALLY. This is really shitty.

CAROL. I know.

ALLY. Was I a bad daughter?

CAROL. Oh my God.

ALLY. He only got to see Max *once*. I hadn't seen him in two years.

CAROL. He didn't make the effort either, Ally. It's not all on you. You always feel so *responsible*, maybe he should have picked up the phone and called you once in a while.

(*pause*)

Here, you know what? I know what will help.

ALLY. What?

> (**CAROL** *exits momentarily, returning with a cardboard box. She puts it on the ground.*)

ALLY. What is that?

CAROL. I was supposed to do this earlier today, I'm going to have to run it to the funeral home tomorrow morning. You can help me pick it out.

> (**CAROL** *starts taking men's clothing out of the box.*)

ALLY. Oh, God, I don't know if I can do this.

CAROL. Take a deep breath. It'll help you out, seriously.

> (**ALLY** *picks up a shirt.*)

ALLY. Oh my God. I remember this one, he was still wearing this?!

CAROL. He never got new clothes. I bought them for him, he wouldn't even wear them.

> (**ALLY** *holds up the shirt.*)

ALLY. He was wearing this that time I broke my leg in high school. God, he drove me to the hospital and / he –

CAROL. It's too bright, I don't like it. I guess the coffin is like a brownish thing, keep that in mind. It's too expensive. What about this?

> (**CAROL** *holds up a white dress shirt for* **ALLY**, *but* **ALLY** *is busy rooting through the box.*)

ALLY. Oh my God!

> (**ALLY** *pulls out a black cape.*)

Do you remember this?! He used to put it on for Halloween every year but he wouldn't wear anything else, it was just this stupid cape and like jeans and a t-shirt or something.

CAROL. What are we gonna bury him in a cape?! Put that back.

ALLY. *(laughing)* No one knew if he was supposed to be a vampire, or a superhero, or Phantom of the Opera –

(**CAROL** *grabs the cape out of* **ALLY***'s hands, throws it back in the box.*)

CAROL. You gonna help me with this or are you gonna help me with this?!

ALLY. Geez. Sorry.

CAROL. He looked like an idiot in this thing anyway. Shouldn't have made it for him.

(*rooting through the box*)

What is this, *silk*?! When did that man ever wear silk?!

(*pause*)

ALLY. Mom?

CAROL. What?

ALLY. What was he wearing when he – …?

(**CAROL** *looks up at her.*)

CAROL. Oh for Jeessum sake.

ALLY. Could you just tell me?

CAROL. No, this is weird. You're weird.

ALLY. *Mom.*

(**CAROL** *sighs, throwing up her hands, starts rooting through the box.*)

CAROL. Dead man's clothes, *that's* crazy. All I did was paint a house white.

(**CAROL** *pulls out a red flannel shirt and a pair of jeans, throws them on the couch.*)

There, that was the outfit. And we're not burying him in this, we are *not* burying him in jeans, that's disgusting.

(**ALLY** *goes to the couch, clears it of everything except the flannel shirt and the jeans. She starts to lay the shirt and the jeans out on the couch.*)

ALLY. Was this where he was sitting?

CAROL. What is wrong with you?

ALLY. I just want to know what it looked like!

CAROL. Why?

ALLY. Because my Dad died and I don't feel anything, okay?! I just want to know what it looked like so maybe I can – … I don't know, I don't know what I'm doing.

> *(ause)*

CAROL. Yes, that's where he was sitting.

> (**ALLY** *lays out the clothes, the shirt on the back of the couch and the jeans on the bottom; the position of a person sitting in the center of the couch.*)

> (*When she finishes,* **ALLY** *stands up and looks at it.*)

ALLY. You were sitting at the table?

CAROL. Yes. What?

ALLY. Go sit down.

CAROL. What is this, a re-enactment? We could call the funeral home and have them bring over the body.

ALLY. Just do it.

> (**CAROL**, *petulant, sits at the table.*)

> (**ALLY** *stands back, looking at the whole stage. Silence.*)

He was breathing…

> *(pause)*

Then he wasn't.

> *(pause)*

He was breathing…

> *(pause)*

Then he wasn't.

> (**BO** *enters from the bedroom, sees* **ALLY**.)

> (*Silence for a moment.* **BO** *watches the two of them.*)

CAROL. Get a glass, Bo.

(Pause. **BO** *considers, he exits to the kitchen, returns with a glass.)*

BO. You shouldn't be drinking.

CAROL. Yeah, well.

*(***CAROL*** pours him a drink, hands it to him.* **ALLY** *continues to look at the clothes on the couch.)*

We're figuring out what to bury him in.

BO. I thought you were having him cremated.

ALLY. *(to* **CAROL***)* You were? Dad always said he didn't want to be cremated.

CAROL. You made such a stupid fuss about it, I called the funeral home, I'm having him cremated. The stupid coffin is going to cost more than his car, I told that to the idiot funeral director, he just kept saying "these are normal prices, Mrs. Nester" in this little voice, he's such a weenie.

(takes a drink)

I don't know why your father always had to tell you kids he didn't want to be cremated, what was wrong with him?

BO. He didn't have any suits?

CAROL. What does he need a suit for?

*(***BO*** drinks.)*

BO. What is this?

CAROL. Oh you know, whatever Dad used to drink. There's a whole box of it in the basement.

BO. It's awful.

CAROL. It's liquor, it's not supposed to taste good.

*(***ALLY*** gets her glass, joins them.)*

ALLY. How was Dad doing this past year or so?

CAROL. What do you mean?

BO. Was he sick?

CAROL. No.

ALLY. Was he drinking a lot?

CAROL. Oh stop. A person dies, that's what a person does. He was fine, he was healthy. He was working fifty hours a week till the day he died.

ALLY. He was a good guy.

CAROL. Okay.

ALLY. Really – special.

CAROL. What was so special about him?

BO. Mom.

CAROL. What? I'm not disrespecting the man, I'm just – . I mean I loved him, I'm not saying I didn't love him. But "special"? Come on. He was a janitor at a hospital for forty-six years.

BO. He had some good stories though.

CAROL. Ugh, all those blood and guts stories, I blame him for you running off to these ridiculous countries, you know.

BO. No, I don't know, what do you mean?

CAROL. You used to pull these disgusting stories out of him, severed limbs and car accidents and whatever. You lapped it up. No wonder you're off taking pictures of all that stuff.

BO. It's really not the same thing, Mom. I'm a journalist.

CAROL. Okay Mr. Smarty.

BO. You really think I'm doing what I'm doing because Dad used to tell us gross stories about the hospital? I've won awards.

CAROL. Well then!

BO. No, I mean – . I'm not saying *I'm* all important or whatever, I'm just saying that what I do – it's journalism. If people like me weren't off in these places taking these pictures, Americans could just be complacent about everything going / on in the rest of –

ALLY. Oh boy, here's the speech.

BO. What, you're on her side?

ALLY. No, but you don't need to get up on some liberal high horse about America.

BO. I'm not on any horse, I just want to establish here that what I'm doing doesn't have anything to do with some adolescent fascination with gore.

(*Pause.* **ALLY** *and* **CAROL** *don't say anything.*)

Oh my God.

CAROL. How about we change the subject?

ALLY. Okay, so you would say that what you do is try to wake up America by showing them the "truth" or something, right?

BO. Well it's not printed on my business card that way, but yes, essentially.

ALLY. So there's no part of you that has any morbid fascination with this stuff?

BO. I don't even know what that means –

ALLY. *Do you get a thrill out of it?*

(*pause*)

BO. I mean – . I don't take *pleasure* in it, if that's what you mean. But yeah, I guess there's a thrill.

ALLY. Alright, that's all I'm getting at. We're done.

BO. Okay, fine, I don't even know what – …

(*pause*)

"Liberal high horse"?

ALLY. What?

BO. You said "liberal high horse," why did you qualify it like that?

CAROL. Back and forth, back and forth! Twenty years ago it was about who ate the Easter candy, now it's this nonsense!

ALLY. Forget it.

BO. No, really.

ALLY. You were just getting all down on Americans, it was pissing me off!

BO. But you used the word "liberal" in that way, that annoying way where you say it like you're saying a bad word or something. Like – *liberal.*

ALLY. Oh my God, can we stop?

BO. Are you getting all conservative now?

ALLY. I'm a business owner, Bo, I know for freelancers like you it's easy to believe whatever you want but for business owners like me there are certain economic realities, certain things / that –

BO. But you don't like vote Republican, do you?

　　　　(response)

　　WHAT?!

CAROL. New topic! New topic!

ALLY. Why is this any of your business?

BO. *(petulant)* No, I am not sleeping in this house unless she admits to us *right now* who she voted for in the last two presidential elections.

CAROL. New topic! Anything you want! Talk about how bat-shit-crazy Mom painted everything white!

ALLY. I am a *business owner*, Bo, and as a business / owner –

　　　　*(**CAROL** exits.)*

BO. You know, you keep saying this, but I'm not really sure what that means, that doesn't prove your point. "I'm a business owner, therefore we should all be Republicans and let the top one percent live in mansions while poor people starve."

ALLY. Yes, you're right, that's what I'm saying. I just hate poor people! Stupid dirty fucking poor people, I hate them!

CAROL. *(offstage)* DON'T USE THAT WORD.

ALLY. YOU SWEAR ALL THE TIME! YOU JUST SAID "BAT-SHIT" LIKE FIVE SECONDS AGO.

CAROL. *(offstage)* IT'S DIFFERENT THAN THE F-WORD.

BO. You're a lesbian! You can't be a Republican lesbian, that doesn't exist! You don't even exist!

ALLY. This has nothing to do with me being a lesbian! It's about personal responsibility!

BO. Oh personal responsibility? Even though the Republican party is controlled completely by hyper-evangelical idiots who believe that the earth is six thousand years old and that women shouldn't be allowed to have an abortion if they were raped by their uncle –

(**CAROL** *re-enters with Christmas decorations.*)

CAROL. CHRISTMAS TIME! IT'S CHRISTMAS TIME, EVERYBODY'S HAPPY!

(*sings loudly*)

HARK THE HERALD ANGELS SING
[ETC.]

(**CAROL** *continues singing over their argument, decorating the room.*)

ALLY. I employ eight people, Bo, these are people that I have taken from half-way homes, from prison release programs, because I believe that I can give them the tools to be responsible citizens, to actually contribute something to society without letting them just bounce from welfare check to welfare check – MOM.

BO. Which is great, no one is saying that isn't great! But guess who are the ones putting social programs into place?! LIBERALS! Because Republicans have jammed our prisons with so many nonviolent drug offenders –

ALLY. Oh Republicans did that? *Republicans* did that, single-handedly?

BO. If it was up to them, they'd have us in a fucking caste system, all the fat cats controlling everything and all the poor people and black people shoved into ghettos –

ALLY. OH MY GOD CAN YOU EVEN *HEAR* YOURSELF?! What does this have to do with race?!

BO. MOM.

CAROL. *(switching songs)*
> DECK THE HALLS WITH BOUGHS OF HOLLY,
> FA LA LA LA LA
> [ETC.]

ALLY. There are things about the Republican party that I don't like, Bo, I'm sure there are things about the Democratic party that you don't like either. But the point is, I believe in *personal responsibility*.

BO. Oh, personal responsibility, personal responsibility, / blah blah blah –

CAROL. Drinks for everybody! Everybody's happy! /
> SILENT NIGHT, HOLY NIGHT
> [ETC.]

> > (**CAROL** *takes the bottle, pours the remainder of the bottle into their three glasses.*)

ALLY. Yes, personal responsibility, because *that* is how you actually help people, not by handing them checks for nothing, not by shoving them into projects, it's by giving them the tools to help *themselves*.

BO. But Republicans aren't even about that anymore! They're just about making sure that the top one percent continues to control fifty perfect of our / economy –

ALLY. You look at me and you ask me how I can be a Republican and a lesbian? The better question is, how can you be a liberal and actually claim to have real compassion for people? Better yet, how can you call yourself a liberal and have ANY CAPACITY FOR CRITICAL THOUGHT?!

BO. *(about to explode, unable to compose a thought)* CRITICAL – ?! YOU HAVE – ?! YOU THINK COMPASSION IS -?!

> > (**CAROL** *smashes the bottle on the floor, shattering it. The room falls silent.*)

> > (*A dog is heard barking outside. Everyone is still,* **BO** *and* **ALLY** *both looking at* **CAROL**.)

*(The dog continues to bark. Finally, **CAROL** exits momentarily, returning with a BB gun. She opens the window and shoots the gun. The dog yips, then is silent. She closes the window. She looks at them for a few more seconds.)*

CAROL. Okay? We're all – ? Okay.

*(**CAROL** exits momentarily. She returns with a dustpan and a broom. She bends down and begins to clean up the broken bottle.)*

I know you think it's fine for you to get at one another like this because now you're older and you've read the paper a few times and think you're all smart or something. But it's the same stupid argument. So just cut it out.

(silence)

BO. Sorry, Mom.

ALLY. Yeah, sorry –

CAROL. Don't be sorry, just don't be idiots.

*(**CAROL** finishes cleaning up the glass, then exits with the dustpan and brush. A moment of silence, **ALLY** and **BO** don't look at one another.)*

BO. Sorry, I – . You're allowed to believe whatever you want.

(pause)

You didn't vote for Bush *twice*, though, right?

ALLY. Oh my God, Bo, stop.

*(**CAROL** returns.)*

CAROL. We all better? We get it out of our systems?

BO. Yes, / Mom.

ALLY. Yeah, I think so.

CAROL. Okay then.

*(**CAROL** goes back to the table, picks up her drink.)*

CAROL. You two, I swear. One time when you were eight and you were five, I had to spray you with the kitchen sink hose just to get you to stop. You remember that?

BO & ALLY. No.

CAROL. Well, it happened. *The kitchen sink hose,* I'm telling you.

> *(**CAROL** takes a long drink.)*

ALLY. You didn't spray us with a hose, c'mon.

CAROL. Your father videoed the whole thing, I can prove it to you if you want. It's in one of those boxes in there.

> *(**CAROL** takes another long drink.)*

BO. Mom why don't you slow down?

CAROL. Again with the drinking.

> *(**CAROL** goes to the box, starts taking out some clothes.)*

This is what we're burying him in.

> *(She throws some khakis and a mustard yellow dress shirt on the couch.)*

Executive decision. Done.

ALLY. Mom, we can't bury him in this.

> *(**ALLY** picks up the shirt.)*

CAROL. Why the hell not?

ALLY. C'mon, it's gross, it's stained.

BO. We can go get him a suit tomorrow first thing, don't worry about it.

CAROL. You're going to *buy a suit?* To *bury in the ground?*

BO. It's fine.

ALLY. We'll take care of it Mom, we can go into Moscow tomorrow and pick up / some –

CAROL. Oh well fine just leave me out then.

BO. You can come, we were just trying / to –

CAROL. You were just trying to what?

(**CAROL** *takes another long drink, finishing the glass.*)

BO. Okay, that's it. Mom, where's the box of liquor?

CAROL. Why?!

BO. I'm getting rid of it.

CAROL. The hell you are! We bought that case last year at the Costco, it cost us more than two hundred bucks!

ALLY. Mom.

CAROL. *I'm* the adult, you understand?! Me!

ALLY. We're all adults now!

(**BO** *heads toward the basement, almost out of the room.*)

CAROL. OKAY OKAY OKAY.

(**BO** *stops, looks at* **CAROL**.)

Okay. Let's talk about this like adults. We're all adults? We can talk about this like adults.

(*pause*)

Please would you take a seat sir?

(**BO** *relents, sits down on the couch.*)

Now. We are going to have an adult conversation about this alcohol thing because you're both driving me up the wall about it. Shall we begin? Ally, sit down.

ALLY. Mom, I don't –

CAROL. *Carol.* You're an adult, I'm an adult, I guess the fact that I pushed you both out of my own body means nothing to you. Just call me Carol.

BO. Oh my God.

CAROL. Now to the matter of this drinking. When you kids were younger, I may have drank too much. I was never an alcoholic because addiction doesn't exist, but I drank too much. And when Dad asked me to stop, I stopped. Right?

(*pause*)

ALLY. Yes.

CAROL. Now while I was under the influence of this alcohol did I ever hit either of you?

BO. No.

CAROL. Did I ever drink and drive and run over people?

BO. No.

CAROL. Alright then.

BO. But you *did* drive Dad's golf cart into the front yard and light it on fire.

CAROL. Exactly, I was a fun person. And besides, I told him I was going to do it if he kept driving it over my tomato plants, he knew it was coming. Point number two! It would be one thing if we had any sort of relationship with each other, but we don't have that, so you have no right to tell me what I can and can't drink.

ALLY. What do you mean we "don't have a relationship"?

CAROL. See now we're talking like adults! The three of us barely know one another anymore.

> *(to* **BO***)*

You're always off in some stupid country or something –

> *(to* **ALLY***)*

and you're a couple hours down the highway but I've barely ever even *met* my grandson. I'm sure you go around telling all your lesbian trucker friends that I some stupid idiot or something –

ALLY. MOM I AM NOT A TRUCKER. I OWN A PRIVATE / TRANSPORTATION -

CAROL. – telling them that it was so wonderful that you got out of stupid little Viola, Idaho, that you're such an enlightened lesbian now, that you don't have time to let your mother see her own grandson.

ALLY. Okay, Mom –

CAROL. *Carol.* We're adults, remember?

ALLY. I know I haven't brought Max over a lot, but –

CAROL. Once. I've seen him – once. Once.

(pause)

Your father just died and you couldn't even bring him over here.

(pause)

ALLY. I'm sorry.

CAROL. Who's sorry? No one's sorry, we're just adults!

(to **BO***)*

And you, I suppose you think you're all important running off to some war torn country, you waltz in there with your camera like you own the place – oh look at the American with the camera! He's a journalist, he's so important! God forbid you actually bend down to help these dying kids or whatever, you just stand there snapping pictures of them, and then you come back to little Viola, Idaho with your pictures of dead little boys and you think you're all enlightened, like you're off doing God's work or whatever, I know something you all don't know, I know what's best, *I really think you should stop drinking.*

*(***CAROL*** goes to the clothes, puts them back in the box.)*

We're cremating him, I just decided. I don't care what you think.

*(***CAROL*** grabs the box of clothes, heads toward the exit.)*

I'm putting these out for the trash man.

ALLY. Mom – don't, please –

CAROL. What, are you gonna wear them?

ALLY. Look, we get it, okay?! Bo and I are sorry –

BO. No I'm not.

*(***CAROL*** looks at* **BO***.)*

CAROL. Oh?

BO. I've got nothing to be sorry about.

(pause)

If you *really* wanna talk Mom, we can talk, I'm fine with that.

ALLY. C'mon, Bo –

BO. I know that you're having fun getting drunk, telling us off –

CAROL. Oh I'm having a *great time.*

BO. And I know that you get to act like some poor wounded animal because we don't visit you enough –

CAROL. Oh, I'm a poor wounded animal!

BO. But guess what Mom?! We're not responsible for your happiness!

CAROL. WHO THE HELL SAID YOU WERE RESPONSIBLE FOR MY HAPPINESS?! I JUST DON'T WANT YOU TO GET ON ME ABOUT MY DRINKING!

BO. Adnd guess what?! Maybe my work *is* important, what about that?! Every time I talk to you on the phone you tell me that I need to stop going to these "awful countries," and you act like it's because you *care* about me, but actually it's because you *can't stand* the thought that I'm actually *doing* something with my life.

> *(pause)*

CAROL. And why is that?

> *(pause)*

Go ahead and say it. "Because you never did anything with yours," is that what you were going to say? Because me and your father are just poor little simpletons, is that it?

BO. I didn't say that –

CAROL. But that's what you meant, isn't it?

BO. No, / it's –

CAROL. Yes it is. Yes, it is.

> *(Silence. **BO** and **CAROL** stare at one another.)*

ALLY. Okay, guys. It's done, we're done talking.

(CAROL continues to stare at BO for a moment, then exits very briefly. She returns with a video cassette, goes to the camera on top of the television, puts the tape inside.)

BO. What is that?

(pause)

Mom. What is that?

(CAROL presses play.)

(An image of MARTIN appears on the screen, as before. He sits facing the camera.)

(CAROL exits without looking at BO or ALLY.)

MARTIN. *(on video)* It's – it's December 12th, I think? Is it?

(no response)

Carol?

(ALLY and BO stand back, watching the television.)

(on video) Are you not even going to talk / to me?

CAROL. *(on video, offscreen)* Oh would you just talk?

MARTIN. *(on video)* What?

CAROL. *(on video, offscreen)* Talk, I said! Talk!

MARTIN. *(on video)* Well what in heck do you think I'm doing?!

CAROL. *(on video, offscreen)* Look in the camera! Don't look at me, look in the camera!

(MARTIN looks back to the camera.)

MARTIN. *(on video)* Oh geez. Okay, I'm looking into the camera.

(pause)

Anyway, your Mom wants me to talk so I'm talking. So it's – Nembutal, is what it's called, before I left the hospital yesterday I grabbed these little vials of Nembutal, the internet says it's a very popular method, I guess it's painless, you just drift right off, and / I –

CAROL. *(on video, offscreen)* Who signed for them?

(*CAROL enters with a fresh bottle of liquor and a full glass. She sips from the glass, watching the video.*)

MARTIN. (*on video*) What?

CAROL. (*on video, offscreen*) I said WHO SIGNED FOR THEM.

MARTIN. (*on video*) *I don't know what you mean.*

CAROL. (*on video, offscreen*) You said a doctor had to sign for them or whatever –

MARTIN. (*on video*) No I just took 'em –

CAROL. (*on video, offscreen*) YOU JUST TOOK 'EM?

MARTIN. (*on video*) Yeah I just took 'em, what in the heck else / am I – ?

CAROL. (*on video, offscreen*) You said you had to get a doctor to do it!

MARTIN. (*on video*) I didn't say that!

CAROL. (*on video, offscreen*) So you stole them! You just stole them!

MARTIN. (*on video*) ARE WE MAKING A MOVIE OR AREN'T WE?

CAROL. (*on video, offscreen*) THEY'RE GONNA CATCH YOU! YOU'RE AN IDIOT!

MARTIN. (*on video*) THEY'RE NOT GONNA CATCH ME. DON'T CALL ME AN IDIOT.

CAROL. (*on video, offscreen*) YOU'RE AN –

(*The shot cuts to static.* ALLY *and* BO *stare at the screen.*)

(*CAROL moves in further, puts the bottle down.* ALLY *and* BO *turn to her. Silence apart from the static on the television.*)

I wasn't going to tell you, but since we're being all *adult-y.*

(*CAROL goes to the television, turns it off. The static cuts off.*)

CAROL. Ally I saved the box of clothes, I put it in your room. Keep them if you want, I don't need them.

>   (*pause*)

Well?

>   (*Silence.* BO *goes to* CAROL.)

BO. What the fuck did he do?

CAROL. Oh we're bringing out the F-word, well then.

ALLY. Oh my God.

BO. I don't understand, how would – . How did he – ?

CAROL. You heard him, he had some ridiculous drug or something. Took it from the hospital a few weeks ago.

BO. But how did – ? You're telling me he just – injected himself with –

ALLY. How could you let him do this?!

CAROL. Oh you know your father, once he gets an idea in his head.

ALLY. But how did – ?

>   (*pause*)

No, you're full of shit.

CAROL. Oh am I? I'm full of *shit*?!

ALLY. Dad did *not* just – . He couldn't have!

CAROL. Well since you're the expert –

BO. No she's right, a person can't just – . They would have found out with the autopsy, they would have found needle marks on his arms –

CAROL. Autopsy? What, are we on *Law and Order*? You remember that little skinny kid from your class, what's his name?

BO. What?

CAROL. The little skinny kid from your class.

BO. I don't – ? What are you talking about?!

CAROL. WHO WAS THE LITTLE SKINNY KID FROM YOUR CLASS? FROM YOUR CLASS, FROM YOUR CLASS!

BO. *I DON'T KNOW!*

CAROL. Well anyway he's the stupid coroner. Got elected last year, he was the only one who ran. He's gotten himself two DUI's this year already.

ALLY. I can't believe this. I can't believe what I'm hearing.

CAROL. You remember his name?

BO. No, I don't remember his – !

(*short pause*)

It's Clive.

CAROL. *Clive*. That's it, little skinny Clive. His parents used to make those god-awful snow cones at the county fair every summer, you remember that?

BO. MOM.

CAROL. Anyway, Clive comes over here with the ambulance or whatever, they look at him for a second and I tell them he just up and died and they were fine with it.

ALLY. But Mom, why did / he – ?

CAROL. I rode with them, I asked to ride with them, and they took the body downtown to the funeral chapel but I guess Frank was gone for the weekend or something, and they kept telling me that they wanted to take the body to *Moscow* or whatever until Frank was back on Monday, but I just all out refused, I have no idea what these funeral chapels are like over in Moscow and I'm not about to –

ALLY. MOM.

CAROL. *Anyway*, Clive said they needed somewhere to put the body and it's not like I could go down the grocery and ask them to put him in a chest freezer, though we did think about that for a second, but then Clive said that he did all this hunting the week before and he had all these elk carcasses in his garage or whatever, that it was sheltered and cool enough, and so anyway we just stuck him in there with the animals until Monday.

BO. Oh my God.

CAROL. And then Frank came back into town and it all became a little more civilized.

BO. Why are you telling us this?!

CAROL. I guess it's my little attempt at illustrating the reasons why a carefully executed suicide might slip through the cracks around here, I'm just saying.

ALLY. *WHY DID HE DO THIS?*

CAROL. Oh for Jeessum sake.

> (*Pause.* CAROL *takes a long drink.*)

BO. If he was depressed, then why didn't he just –

CAROL. Oh depressed, he was depressed, we should have just given him some pills and he'd be fine, is that it? You're so enlightened Bo, I swear, you're so *enlightened.*

ALLY. Why didn't you call me?! I live three hours away, I could have come down if Dad / was –

CAROL. And what good would you have done? Maybe you could have come down here and guilted him in to living a few more years, but what for?

ALLY. What did he say? Did he tell you why?

CAROL. There are a lot of things you two don't understand.

BO. OKAY THAT'S IT.

> (BO *stands up, exiting offstage. He returns momentarily with his backpack, shoving his clothes and toiletries into it as he talks.*)

CAROL. What do you think you're doing?

BO. I'm leaving.

CAROL. The hell you are!

BO. You can't just – ! You can't bring us here, tell us that Dad killed himself, and then just tell us that "we wouldn't understand." It's so fucking manipulative –

ALLY. Bo.

CAROL. No, he's right. Your brother's right. He's right.

> (BO *stops, looking at* CAROL.)

Bo, you're – . I get it, I see what I'm doing, I can see myself. I'm sorry, okay? I'm sorry.

> (**BO** *looks at her.* **CAROL** *takes her glass of liquor, holding it up. She looks around, then goes to the Christmas tree, pours the remainder of the glass into the Christmas tree stand. She puts the empty glass down.*)

Okay? No more.

> (**BO** *calms down a bit.*)

Now if you really want me to try and explain all this – I'll try and explain. I can do that. It may just make things worse, but – we can try it this way. How about that?

> *(pause)*

CAROL. Let's just – sit down. Family time. What's left of us.

> (**BO** *relents, putting his backpack down and finding a place to sit.* **ALLY** *finds a place to sit as well,* **CAROL** *remains standing.*)

Now the first thing I want you to get out of your heads is any ideas about depression, crazy, whatever. Your father's brain – and mine – was and is doing just fine. Alright?

> (**CAROL** *exits momentarily, continuing to talk.*)

(offstage) I know that nowadays we all like to explain away everything in life by putting some stupid word next to it – depression, bi-polar, schizo-whatever – but we're not talking about that, we are talking about *reason*. Alright? *Reason.*

> (**CAROL** *re-enters with two or three of the Costco snack trays. She tosses one to* **BO** *and* **ALLY**.*)

ALLY. Mom when someone kills themselves, that means that something *is* wrong with their brain. Someone doesn't / just –

CAROL. Oh shut up with your stupid psychology. Your father *arrived* at this decision, it wasn't something he just came up with last week, he had been thinking about it for years.

BO. *Years?*

CAROL. YES YEARS. LISTEN TO MY MOUTH. YEARS, YEARS.

(**CAROL** *opens up a snack tray, eats a bit.*)

ALLY. Why?!

CAROL. Well once you kids left I guess he just sorta realized who he was, his place in – . Okay. Listen to me.

(**CAROL** *stands up with the snacktray.*)

Now I don't know if you even know about this but apparently our entire universe came out of some big explosion or something, and ever since then, all these stars and planets and whatever –

(*grabbing a cracker*)

– have just been spiraling out into nothingness –

(**CAROL** *throws the cracker to a corner of the room, then grabs more crackers and continues to throw them around the room.*)

– and these things that used to be one thing are now just spiraling out into the depths of space or something. And then you've got our little planet –

(**CAROL** *takes a cracker, holds it up.*)

– that actually has *life* on it.

(**CAROL** *takes a piece of salami, puts it on top of the cracker.*)

This one special little stupid piece of dirt that has all these people on it, and we're all *very impressed* with ourselves, living on this little planet, but if you actually think about it?

(**CAROL** *grabs an unopened snack tray.*)

We all just came from the same little stupid speck of whatever. Everything, everything you know about people, time, history, your dirty laundry – it's all just from this same little thing. *The same stupid little snack tray.*

(**CAROL** *drops the snack tray on the ground,
looking at* **BO** *and* **ALLY**.)

Get it?

(*pause*)

BO. You're saying that Dad killed himself because of the
big bang?

CAROL. Yeah! Not *just* that, that just sort of – led him to
the idea. After you both left we had all this *time* on our
hands, and we started reading all these book, and we –

ALLY. What books?

CAROL. *Books*, I don't know. Years ago he saw some program
on public television about the big bang and whatever,
so he found a few books and we both read them and
started getting interested in all that stuff.

ALLY. When did Dad ever read a *book*? Do you guys even
own any books?

(*pause*)

CAROL. Oh you're right, we didn't go to *college* so I guess
we're both as dumb as dirt, is that it?

ALLY. I'm not saying that, I'm just saying – I never even saw
him read a *newspaper* let / alone –

CAROL. You sit there barking at me, talking to me like I'm
some idiot, like I'm – . I know you'd like to believe that
we're just some stupid simpletons, but your father was
a real person. A real person who started to understand
who he was, his place in – everything. And rather than
spending the rest of his life wiping floors at a hospital
and wasting away in this house, he released himself
into the universe. The most beautiful, meaningful
thing he's ever done.

(*pause*)

I'm going to bed. Turn out the lights when you're done.

(**CAROL** *gets up and exits, taking the bottle of
liquor with her.* **ALLY** *and* **BO** *sit for a moment,
silent.*)

BO. What are we – ? I don't know what we're supposed to do with this.

>   (*pause*)

That stupid fucking asshole, why did he do this?!

ALLY. I have to go to bed, I can't even think. I don't even know what's going on.

BO. And what the hell did Dad ever know about *science*? He never even watched an episode of *Star Trek*, what the hell does he know about science?

>   (*pause*)

I just don't – . After all this time, suddenly the man has an inner life? When the hell did that happen?

>   (**BO** *opens up a snack tray, eats a few bites. Silence.*)

ALLY. Do you think – …?

BO. What?

ALLY. He didn't do this because of us, did he?

>   (*pause*)

BO. Because of *us*?

ALLY. You know, because we – . I don't know, we never visited, or –

BO. This is not on us, Ally. I refuse to take any of the blame for this. He was a distant, nonexistent father to us our entire lives.

ALLY. Yeah.

>   (*pause*)

BO. Ally.

>   (*no response*)

Ally.

>   (**ALLY** *finally looks at him.*)

You know this wasn't our fault, right?

ALLY. I know, I know.

BO. He was just – sick, I guess.

> (**CAROL** *returns, with the bottle of liquor and some video tapes in her hands. She stumbles into the room, obviously much drunker than a moment ago.*)

Mom.

CAROL. *Well hello.*

ALLY. Mom, c'mon, go to bed, it's late.

BO. Mom you need to stop, give me the bottle.

CAROL. I just had a few little more nightcaps.

> (**CAROL** *stumbles into the room,* **BO** *takes the bottle from her.*)

BO. C'mon, let's go to bed.

CAROL. No I just had something to tell you so quick. Okay? I'll be so quick, I just.

ALLY. Jesus.

CAROL. Now first of all I wanted to give you these to you.

> (**CAROL** *drops the tapes onto the floor.*)

They're tapes of Dad, I had him make you these tapes to try and explain everything, why he did this, whatever. So just watch the tapes and you'll learn so much.

BO. Great.

ALLY. Thank you, Mom.

CAROL. ALSO. I just wanted to let you both know that I'm planning on doing the same thing as your father after the funeral tomorrow just so you know. And I'd like you both to help me with it.

> (*pause*)

BO. Wait, what?

CAROL. He saved me some of the drug he used and I'm going take it tomorrow, just like him. So it's good that everything in the house is white, you won't have to worry about selling all of the *stuff*, because it's all white anyway, so after I die you can just throw it all out and just sell the house and be done with it. I've made it very easy for both of you.

(quick pause)

YOU'RE WELCOME.

(black)

End of Act One

ACT TWO

Scene One

(The television flips on, a shot of **MARTIN** *appears on the television)*

MARTIN. *(on video)* – which is really just an effort to negotiate ideas of, uh. Relativity, and – you know, Einstein's relativity –

CAROL. *(on video, offscreen)* Ugh.

MARTIN. *(on video)* – and uh, quantum mechanics, which sort of seem like they're in opposition / to one another –

CAROL. *(on video, offscreen)* Martin, you don't have to run your mouth off about whatever, just tell them what String Theory is!

(Lights rise on the living room, the next morning. **BO** *sits watching the television.)*

MARTIN. *(on video)* You know Carol if *you* wanna do this, I'm fine with / that –

CAROL. *(on video, offscreen)* Talk about the strings! Just get through it!

MARTIN. *(on video)* Okay. So people are thinking that these strings are the basic building block of everything around us –

*(**ALLY** enters, holding a book.)*

ALLY. Hey.

BO. Hey.

MARTIN. *(on video)* – it's smaller than any other thing we know – smaller than atoms, smaller than quarks –

(BO turns off the camera, the television shuts off.)

ALLY. Merry Christmas.

BO. Oh my God. It's Christmas morning, isn't it?

ALLY. Yeah. Pretty shitty Christmas, even for this house.
You check on Mom?

BO. She's fine. Still asleep. She'll be asleep for a while
probably. I looked everywhere for the – whatever.

ALLY. Nembutal.

BO. Yeah. Bathroom, her bedroom – I can't find it.

(re: the book)

What's that?

ALLY. I found it in a box outside this morning. Mom left it
out for the trash man.

BO. What is it?

ALLY. It's about Quantum Mechanics. There are notes on
almost every page.

*(**ALLY** shows the book to **BO**.)*

There are more out there, too.

*(**BO** skims through the book, tosses it back down on
the couch.)*

BO. Hm.

ALLY. So?

(pause)

BO. What?

*(**ALLY** stares at him.)*

What I said?

ALLY. I don't know, Bo, I – .

(pause)

He didn't seem – sick. Or crazy. Mom doesn't seem sick
or crazy.

BO. You're telling me that Mom doesn't seem crazy? After
last night?

ALLY. She was drunk.

BO. I think a double suicide counts as crazy, Ally. Should we call the – police? I don't know, who do you call when someone is crazy? The hospital?

ALLY. Wait – what do you mean?

BO. Well I don't know, I don't know how you – commit someone, I don't know how to do that. Do I call the, like – asylum? Is that what it's called?

(**BO** *goes to an end table, taking out a phone book.*)

ALLY. What are you doing?

BO. I'm just – I'm just looking.

ALLY. You're looking up "asylums" in the fucking phone book?!

BO. Well I don't know! At least I'm doing something!

ALLY. You're a retard!

BO. *You're* a re-!

(*catching himself*)

Oh my God, how old are we?

(**BO** *throws the phone book back into the end table.*)

ALLY. You can't just – . You can't just *commit* her, Bo, it's not the 19th century.

BO. She's threatening to kill herself.

ALLY. Okay so, say we make her go to the hospital, and she gets interviewed by a psychiatrist or whatever – you really think she's dumb enough to actually *tell* them that she's planning on killing herself? All she has to say is that we're lying.

BO. What, so you want to just *wait around* until she kills herself?!

ALLY. No I'm not *okay* with it, I'm just – . What, are we gonna strap her down at night, pump her full of thorazine during the day?

BO. *Dear God, every time I come home.* I walk into this house and it's like every bit of reason, every shred of rationality just flies right out the window. At least being in a country at war, you know what the hell is going on, you understand people's motivations, but in this house?!

ALLY. Well maybe if you'd get off of your high horse for a / second –

BO. My *liberal* high horse.

ALLY. Maybe if you just got off it, you'd realize that some people just feel completely – *alone*, some people really don't have any reason to move from day to day, some people don't –

> (**ALLY** *stops, looks at* **BO**, *red-faced. She suddenly looks down, putting her face in her hands.* **BO** *stares at her. Silence.*)

BO. What are you – ? What are you doing?

> (**ALLY** *doesn't move.*)

Are you crying?

> (*pause*)

Holy shit. You're crying.

> (*Silence.* **BO** *is motionless,* **ALLY** *continues to cry into her hands silently.*)

Do you want like – a hug?

> (**BO**, *not knowing what to do, gets up, moves to* **ALLY**. *He awkwardly puts his arms around her. As soon as his arms touch her:*)

ALLY. GET THE FUCK OFF BO.

BO. *Sorry*, I don't know what to – …!

> (*pause*)

Sorry.

> (**ALLY** *starts to regain herself.*)

Are you – sad about Mom?

ALLY. Shut up.

BO. Is it Dad?

ALLY. No, it's – …

>*(pause)*

Laura and Max left.

>*(pause)*

BO. What do you mean?

ALLY. Me. They left me. Laura left and she took Max with her. I'm not even sure where she went, I think she might be with her cousin in Seattle.

BO. What happened?

ALLY. *That's just the thing, nothing happened, nothing –* .

>*(pause)*

She just kept saying that I don't spend enough time at home, that I don't spend enough time around Max, or – . I don't know. She's just – crazy, that's what it is. She's crazy.

BO. She left the state and took your kid with her because she doesn't feel like you spend enough time at home?

ALLY. I know! She's crazy!

>*(pause)*

I mean I work a lot, but it's for them! I do it for them!

BO. How much do you work?

ALLY. I don't know.

BO. You get weekends off though, right?

ALLY. Yeah right, I wish. Weekends. We have double the amount of runs to the airport on weekends, I'm usually doing some of the driving myself, not to mention all the courier deliveries we have / for the –

BO. You don't take *any* days off?

ALLY. I own a business! Every day I'm directing thirty-six twelve-passenger vans and –

BO. What time do you get home usually?

ALLY. I don't know – eleven? Midnight, I guess?

BO. Are you serious?

ALLY. *I own the second largest fleet of passenger vehicles in northern / Idaho –*

BO. OKAY okay. You just sound – busy. That's a long work week.

ALLY. I mean I get Thanksgiving and Christmas off, and – . Goddammit.

> (**ALLY** *buries her head in her hands.*)

I just don't get it. We have money, two-story house on thirty acres. She has her own organic garden, Max has anything he could ever want. I don't know when this – stopped working.

BO. Look, business is good, right?

ALLY. Yeah.

BO. So hire a manager or something. You can delegate some of this stuff, can't you?

ALLY. Bo this thing took me *ten years* to build, I'm not hiring some idiot who's gonna screw it all up.

BO. But you do realize that most people don't have that kind of work week. Especially people with a one-year-old.

ALLY. HE'S TWO, BO. MY SON IS TWO YEARS OLD.

BO. SORRY. Sorry.

> (*pause*)

ALLY. It's also that – …

> (**ALLY** *trails off.*)

BO. What?

ALLY. Look don't get all weird when I say this, but *maybe, sometimes* I feel a little like – we shouldn't have had a kid.

> (*silence*)

BO. Whoa.

ALLY. Not like – *all the time*, I just.

> (*pause*)

Look it's not like I don't love him, I love him more than anything, that's *why* I feel like maybe we should have – . I mean, look at what this kid is being born into. Global warming, a collapsing economy, countries exploding, Islamic fanatics trying to take over the country –

BO. Okay you can't actually believe that Muslims are trying to / take over –

ALLY. SHUT UP I DON'T CARE IF YOU THINK I'M RACIST SHUT UP.

    (pause)

Anyway. I'm just saying, that we seem to have brought a new life into this world at a pretty screwed up time, and – . Do you realize that by the time he's my age, it's going to be the year 2042? Are we even going to *make* it that far? Who the fuck are *we* to bring another life into the world, right now? What are we even thinking?

    (pause)

And so I get to thinking about all of this stuff, and it just seems like I should *prepare* in some way, that if I'm a responsible parent I really should have some sort of plan if – whatever happens, you know? So I get some money together to build a shelter, just in case something were to happen, and Laura got all angry at because I didn't tell her about it, but I / was just –

BO. What do you mean a "shelter"? What does that mean?

ALLY. You know, like – in case anything happens. Like an underground shelter, like a bunker. I know it sounds crazy, but when you really consider what could happen in the next twenty years it's really / not –

BO. How much is it costing you?

ALLY. There's a company in Eastern Washington that does this stuff, they get really good prices, I did my homework. And I'm taking care of a lot of the installation myself, they just send the basic structure and / I'm –

BO. How much will it cost?

ALLY. I have a payment plan, I just – .

> *(pause)*

A little under fifty thousand, okay?

BO. Holy *shit*, Ally.

ALLY. *Shut up.*

BO. You spent fifty thousand dollars and you didn't tell your *wife*?

ALLY. She would've gotten all weird about it!

BO. Yeah because it's crazy!

ALLY. Do you know how much shit is going on right now?! How many different ways this whole fucking country could just blow up right in our / faces –

BO. Oh right, because things have *never* been this bad, right? Ally, terrible things have always happened. Economic meltdowns, epidemics, war, genocide, whatever – it's been going on since forever, and will continue to go on forever, and the world isn't gonna blow up anytime soon. God, everyone in this country is so fucking obsessed with themselves that they have to manufacture this apocalypse bullshit because their lives are so boring / that they –

ALLY. OH MY GOD I DON'T NEED THE SPEECH.

> *(pause)*

Just forget it, nevermind.

> *(pause)*

BO. You want some coffee?

> *(pause)*

ALLY. Yeah.

> **(BO** *exits momentarily.)*

BO. *(offstage, from the kitchen)* Have you tried just giving her a call?

> **(ALLY** *doesn't respond.)*

(offstage) I SAID –

ALLY. I HEARD YOU SHUT UP.

> (**BO** *re-enters with two cups of coffee, hands one to* **ALLY**.)

BO. So?

> (*silence*)

ALLY. Maybe I shouldn't.

> (*pause*)

BO. What do you mean?

ALLY. Just, I don't know. Maybe I shouldn't.

> (**CAROL** *enters in her pajamas, obviously hung over.*)

CAROL. There's coffee?

BO. Yeah.

CAROL. Okay. Good morning, Merry Christmas, Merry Christmas.

> (**CAROL** *exits to the kitchen.*)

ALLY. Don't say anything to her about Laura and Max.

BO. Of course I'm not going to say anything. We've got enough to deal with.

> (*pause*)

What did you mean, "maybe I shouldn't"? Why *wouldn't* you call her?

> (*pause*)

ALLY. Forget it.

> (*pause*)

BO. You should call her.

ALLY. I know.

BO. *You should call her.*

ALLY. *I know.*

> (**CAROL** *re-enters with coffee. She goes to the stereo, presses play, Christmas carols begin to play.*)

CAROL. Remind me not to drink that stuff anymore. Your Dad was crazy, that stuff is terrible, gives me hangovers. I'm sticking to my Crème de Menthe.

ALLY. How about *not* drinking, Mom, how about that?

CAROL. You kids, I swear to God. I have one drink too many and it's the Spanish Inquisition! String her up! Guillotine!

> *(pause)*

I won't drink anymore, not while you're here. But it's not because I have a problem, it's because you two are irritating.

> *(re: the music)*

Oh I like this one.

BO. Mom?

> (**CAROL** *doesn't respond, listening to the music.*)

Mom.

CAROL. Ugh. What?

> (**BO** *goes to the music, turns it off.*)

Do you have to turn that off?

BO. Yes.

CAROL. Right, I forgot that it's your job to make sure I don't get any of the things in life that make me feel good. Continue.

> *(Pause.* **BO** *goes to her.)*

BO. We want you to check yourself into the hospital.

CAROL. What?

BO. We think it'd be best, and we don't want to force you, so we want you to check yourself in.

CAROL. What do I need to go to the hospital for?

BO. We don't want you to hurt yourself. We care about you –

CAROL. Ugh.

BO. – and we don't want you to hurt yourself.

CAROL. Who's hurting herself? I'm not hurting myself! I'm drinking coffee!

BO. Where is the drug?

CAROL. What drug?

BO. The drug that Dad used? Where is it?

CAROL. Damn your father's terrible liquor, I never should have told you that. If I just would've stuck to my Crème de Menthe I never would have blabbed.

BO. I already took all of the knives out of the kitchen –

CAROL. What did you do that for?! What did you do with my knives?!

BO. I took them out.

CAROL. Those are expensive knives! They're Swedish or something!

BO. I just – . I just put them somewhere, they're fine. And I hid Dad's old hunting rifles, and took all of the medicine out of the bathroom, but I can't make this house totally safe for you, which is why we really think that you / should –

CAROL. Where did you put my knives?

BO. I'm not telling you.

CAROL. I'll call the police! Where did you put them?!

BO. Mom it's – they're fine!

CAROL. If you gave them to the Goodwill I'm going to buy them back right now and stab you with them.

BO. THIS ISN'T – Mom, I'm trying to have a serious conversation right now, I just hid them because I didn't want you to hurt yourself with them, but this isn't about that, it's –

CAROL. Where did you hide them?!

BO. THEY'RE JUST IN THE BASEMENT SOMEWHERE, OKAY?!

CAROL. THEY'RE GONNA GET RUSTED IN THE BASEMENT!

BO. DEAR GOD PLEASE STOP TALKING ABOUT THE KNIVES! WE JUST WANT YOU TO GO TO THE HOSPITAL, ALRIGHT?! WE WANT YOU TO CHECK YOURSELF IN TO THE HOSPITAL!

ALLY. Bo, could you just – ? You don't have to *scream* at her –

BO. Look are you going to help me, or not?

ALLY. Why can't we just sit down and talk like rational human beings?!

BO. Because she isn't rational! Nothing about this is rational!

ALLY. Oh right because you're so superior and / we're just –

BO. When did I say I was "superior"?!

CAROL. WHAT IN THE HELL DID I SAY TO YOU KIDS LAST NIGHT?!

> *(pause)*

BO. You don't remember what you said to us?

CAROL. I remember spilling the beans about Dad, but what did –…

> *(pause, remembering)*

Oh.

> *(pause)*

GAH your father's liquor.

> (**CAROL** *goes to the stereo, turns the Christmas carols back on.*)

I wasn't planning on telling you kids until after the funeral, I thought we could at least get through that first, but – might as well get it over with anyway.

BO. Do you have the drug? The thing that Dad used?

CAROL. Well of course I have it. It's very peaceful, I guess it's the most popular method among doctors who are suiciders, so it's kinda classy. And it's very peaceful, it won't look ugly or anything. I have it all planned out for you.

(**CAROL** *goes to a drawer, takes out a piece of paper.*)

CAROL. I wrote down all the instructions. I'd like you kids to be around when it actually happens but then you have to leave right away and just go shopping or something, then you come back and you call the police and tell them you found me. It's really simple, I've made it easy.

BO. Mom you realize – we're not going to let you do this. There's no way that we would let you do this.

(*pause*)

CAROL. Did you watch the videos I gave you?

ALLY. We watched some of them.

CAROL. Then I don't know what else you kids want from me, I don't – .

(*pause*)

Okay, how about this? Let's walk through it. I'll walk through it and I'll show you kids that it's not bad at all.

BO. What?

(**CAROL** *goes to the couch, reaching inside of a cushion. She takes out a vial of Nembutal and a syringe.*)

ALLY. Oh my God –

BO. *Mom give that to me right now.*

CAROL. What?! Why should I?!

BO. I don't want you hurting yourself!

CAROL. Are you listening to me?! I'm just going to walk you through it! I'm not doing anything!

ALLY. Mom just give us the – . Just give it to us, please.

CAROL. I'm not giving it to you kids, you'll just drop it or lose it. I'll put it away, okay?

(**CAROL** *puts the vial into her pocket.*)

Okay, so here's how it'll happen. I'll be sitting right here, just like your Dad.

(CAROL sits on the couch.)

CAROL. And I want my Christmas carols to be playing but not this tape, I want the Bing Crosby. Remember that, okay? Write it down on that paper.

ALLY. It's fine –

CAROL. WRITE IT DOWN. YOU'RE GONNA FORGET.

ALLY. I'LL REMEMBER.

CAROL. Anyhoo, I'll be sitting right here like this. And we'll say our goodbyes or whatever and then I'll go like this.

(CAROL puts the syringe up to her arm.)

And I'll inject the stuff into me, and then I'll die. Okay? I'm dying right now, this is me dying.

(CAROL slumps over. Pause.)

Okay so then I'm dead and then you two have to get out of here, you need to just leave for an hour or two. Maybe just an hour, you don't want me smelling up the place. Martin smelled a little bit, I think he may have pooped himself, but I won't do that.

BO. Okay, Mom, we don't need to –

CAROL. I SAID I WON'T POOP MYSELF. *Jessum Crow.* Okay then when you come back here and you have to call the police, you say you just found me like this – and then Clive will come in and he's gonna ask you what happened, and you're gonna tell him that you just found me like this.

(Pause. CAROL looks at BO and ALLY.)

Well?

ALLY. What?

CAROL. Say it. Pretend I'm Clive, tell me what happened. I just want to hear how you'll say it.

BO. No, we are / not –

CAROL. Ally, just say it. Just say "we walked in and found her like this."

(Pause. BO glares at ALLY. ALLY relents.)

ALLY. *(awkward, annoyed)* We walked in and found her like this.

CAROL. THAT'S HOW YOU'RE GONNA SAY IT?

BO. OKAY ENOUGH.

> *(pause)*

This isn't happening. We are not going to do this.

CAROL. Bo, it's really not that bad, you only have a few things that you need to do –

BO. You're not hearing me, Mom – we are not going to help you do this. Neither of us are going to participate in this.

> *(pause)*

Do you know how many dead bodies I've seen, bodies of people who *didn't* want to die, who were *forced* into these situations, and – ? There are a lot of people who would love to have your life right now, and you just giving up, it's – . It's vulgar.

CAROL. Bo I've been thinking this through for years now, nothing you can possibly come up with right now is anything I haven't thought of before. It's not sad, it's not immoral, it's just – what it is. I'm done. Nothing left for me to do. I'm sorry that it seems vulgar to you, but it's – my life. The last thing I have control over. It's not about depression, or pain, or whatever. It's about *my choice.*

> *(pause)*

I helped your Dad, and now – I'd like you to help me.

> (**BO** *and* **ALLY** *are silent.*)

Please.

> *(No response.* **CAROL** *thinks.)*

You kids watch the rest of the tapes from your dad, think about it, and if you still think I'm just stupid – you can just go. You don't have to be here if you don't want to. Up to you.

(**CAROL** *exits.*)

(*The lights snap to black, the TV flickers and begins to play:*)

Home Video

(**MARTIN** *appears on the television, as before.*)

MARTIN. You kids remember when grandpa was in the hospital, right before he died? And I didn't let you see him, I didn't allow you to go to visit with him. And you thought that I was so cruel for doing that, you thought that I was a monster, that I was – ... Carol, you remember that?

CAROL. *(offscreen)* Yeah. I remember.

(*Lights slowly rise on the living room.* **BO** *sits watching the television.*)

MARTIN. He was real thin toward the end. Tubes hooked up to him, barely recognized me. Cancer had gone to his brain, his eyes turned this milky blue and he'd just stare forward, right through you. This guy who fought in World War II, who started his own business from the ground up, and – ... Every day I'd go to work. I'd be mopping the floor right outside his room. I'd pass by it around 3:45 in the morning, and I'd open the door and look at him. Started bringing the camera with me to work, taping him, so I wouldn't forget what he looked like.

(*pause*)

Yesterday I pulled out some of those tapes to remind myself what he looked like. Thing is, these tapes – they don't last forever. Eventually, they just turn to static. You watch them enough, let them sit in a box long enough, they lose the signal. I hadn't watched the thing for years, but I guess I had watched it so many times – the tape was just static.

(*pause*)

I watched it for a while. The whole thing is – just static.

Scene Two

(A few hours later. **ALLY** *enters, sees* **BO**. *A bottle of the liquor sits out,* **BO** *is drinking from a glass.)*

ALLY. Hey. Where were you?

*(***BO*** stops the tape, not looking at ***ALLY***.)*

HELLO?

BO. I didn't feel like going, okay?

ALLY. It was really shitty of you to miss this. There are certain things that people *do* when their parent dies.

BO. Look I'll participate in what I want to participate in, all right?

(pause)

Where's Mom?

ALLY. She's downtown.

BO. Downtown?

ALLY. She just dropped me off. She's getting the flowers for the funeral.

*(***BO*** gets up.)*

BO. And you just – *let her go?*

ALLY. *Yeah,* so what?

BO. So right at this moment, she could be out in the middle of the forest hanging herself from some tree, that's what you're telling me?

ALLY. A TREE? WHAT THE HELL ARE YOU TALKING ABOUT?

BO. Fine. Just let her do whatever she wants, who cares?!

ALLY. She's an adult! I'm not her babysitter!

*(***BO*** drinks.)*

And you're fucking *drinking?*

BO. Yeah, so what?

ALLY. Fine, whatever. Sit back and be totally fucking useless. I'll take care of *everything,* because for some reason it's

my responsibility to cart Mom around and make / sure
—

BO. You know, you're sort of – …

> *(**BO** trails off.)*

ALLY. What?

BO. Nothing.

ALLY. No really, what? What big stupid speech do you have for me now?

BO. You're sort of pathetic sometimes, you know that?

> *(Silence. **ALLY** stares at him.)*

ALLY. I'm sorry, what was that?

BO. I said *you're sort of pathetic sometimes*. And I'm not even talking about you spending tens of thousands of dollars on some underground crazy tank, or voting for Bush. Those things *aside*, you're still sort of just – pathetic. You always just side with Mom and Dad, no matter what. Dad killed himself? Fine with you. Mom wants to do the same thing? Ally has no problem with it! You were always just so fucking – *spineless* with them, I just – …

> *(silence)*

ALLY. No, that's great, keep going.

> *(no response)*

Oh you're done? You can keep going. Because I'll just stand here and listen to you spew your self-righteous bullshit because I'm so *spineless* and *pathetic*. Right?

> *(pause)*

And since I'm so *spineless* and *pathetic*, I won't tell you that when you up and left when you were seventeen, believe it or not you were actually leaving a fourteen-year-old girl in this house *alone with them*. For three years, all their crazy shit that *had* been equally distributed between the two of us was suddenly directed *entirely* at me. Suddenly Dad only had one kid and he had to make sure that every movement I made was on tape –

BO. OKAY.

ALLY. But it's okay because you're some big important photographer, you *really matter*. I however stuck it out here, I waited until college to actually leave –

BO. And then you did exactly what I did, you stopped coming here.

ALLY. I know it's convenient for you to believe that, but I *was* coming back here. For years after I left I still came home for Thanksgiving, Christmas, called Mom every week, all the while building a business with an annual operating budget of over a million dollars.

BO. Oh I'm very impressed, Ally. You live in one of the wealthiest capitalist economies in the world and you managed to create a *business*, it's so impressive. Too bad you don't spend half as much time thinking about your family as you do thinking about your business.

ALLY. What the fuck did you just say to me?

BO. You heard me.

ALLY. Are you saying I'm a bad parent?

BO. No, all good parents spend their kid's college money building apocalypse bunkers and working until midnight every night –

(**ALLY** *punches* **BO** *in the shoulder.*)

Did you just *hit* me?

ALLY. Don't talk to me about my family, I'll kick your ass.

BO. Oh you'll "kick my ass"?

ALLY. I will *break you.*

BO. Oh sure.

ALLY. What, you think I'm fragile? Go ahead.

(**ALLY** *punches* **BO** *again.*)

BO. Alright, you need to stop touching me *right now.*

ALLY. You've spent your whole life in third world countries exploiting other people's misery. How about that?

BO. Oh is that what I've been doing?

ALLY. You're ignorant, childish, self-righteous, *immoral* –

        *(**BO** pushes **ALLY**.)*

BO. How about that?

ALLY. That's great, I like it.

        *(**ALLY** pushes **BO** back, harder.)*

BO. I said don't fucking touch me, Ally. I don't want to hurt you.

ALLY. Oh, you don't want to *hurt* me?

BO. Shut up.

ALLY. Oh big strong man, I'm just a poor widdle / woman!

BO. SHUT UP.

ALLY. Please don't hurt me!

        *(**BO** goes at her, they begin to wrestle for a bit.)*

        *(**ALLY** manages to get the upper hand, pins **BO** down on the ground.)*

OH BIG STRONG MAN WHAT JUST HAPPENED?

BO. YOU'RE REALLY HURTING MY ARM. YOU ARE ACTUALLY HURTING MY ARM.

        *(**ALLY** twists his arm, **BO** screams in pain. Just then, **CAROL** enters, holding a huge potted bouquet of white carnations accented with pink ribbons. She looks at **BO** and **ALLY**, **BO** and **ALLY** don't notice her.)*

ALLY. SAY "I'M A RETARD"! SAY IT!

BO. FUCK YOU!

        *(**ALLY** twists his arm, **BO** cries out in pain. **CAROL** puts down the carnations and exits.)*

OKAY OKAY I'M A RETARD! GET OFF ME!

ALLY. NOW SAY "OBAMA'S A RETARD"!

BO. WHAT?!

ALLY. SAY IT!

        *(**BO** manages to wrestle his way out of her grip and pins her down onto the ground.)*

BO. SAY "I'M A STUPID LITTLE GIRL"!

ALLY. GET OFF ME!

BO. I'M A STUPID LITTLE GIRL!

> (*Just then* **CAROL** *enters with a garden hose trailing behind her. She sprays* **BO** *and* **ALLY**, *they immediately break up, rolling off one another.* **CAROL** *continues to spray them for a moment, then stops.*)

> (**ALLY** *and* **BO** *have begun to laugh uncontrollably on the floor, unable to talk.*)

CAROL. What you're *laughing* now?

> (*pause*)

You're both crazy.

> (**ALLY** *and* **BO** *continue to laugh.* **BO** *notices the white carnations.*)

BO. What – ? What are those?

> (**ALLY** *looks at the flowers.*)

ALLY. Oh my God, what are those?

CAROL. They're for the funeral.

> (**ALLY** *and* **BO** *continue to laugh.*)

ALLY. Why – ? Why are they *white?* They have *pink ribbons!*

CAROL. Glenn the florist made it for some wedding, but the bride didn't want it or something.

BO. That's – ? That's for the *funeral?*

CAROL. It was fifty percent off! What do you want from me?!

> (**BO** *and* **ALLY** *break into another fit of laughter.*)

You two are both crazy.

> (**CAROL** *exits with the hose.*)

> (**ALLY** *and* **BO** *start to calm down, their laughter sudbsides.*)

BO. I didn't hurt you, did I?

ALLY. No, did I hurt *you?*

BO. No, I'm – I'm fine.

>   *(They get up.* **CAROL** *re-enters.)*

CAROL. Alright idiots, are you done with whatever that was?

BO & ALLY. Yeah.

CAROL. Alright then.

>   *(pause)*

You two make a decision yet? Either of you sticking around?

>   *(Pause.* **BO** *and* **ALLY** *don't respond.)*

Well you'll have to decide soon, because I'm doing this right after the funeral.

>   *(***CAROL*** *exits into the kitchen. Pause.)*

BO. What are you gonna do?

ALLY. I'm not going to leave her alone, I'm not gonna…

>   *(pause)*

What are you gonna do?

CAROL. *(offstage)* If you don't want to be here, then all I ask is that you take care of selling the house. You won't make much money off it but you can split it down the middle, or whatever you want.

>   *(***CAROL*** *re-enters with a Christmas-themed tablecloth, four Christmas-themed plates, and a rag to wipe up the water. She cleans any water off of the dining table as she speaks.)*

I don't know where the deed is but Dad says where it is in one of those videos. Like I said, it's all nice and easy. Ally, help me with this?

>   *(***CAROL*** *unfolds the table cloth.)*

ALLY. What are we doing?

CAROL. It's Christmas.

ALLY. Mom, I / don't –

CAROL. Let's have a Christmas.

(**ALLY** *looks at* **BO***, then helps* **CAROL** *spread the tablecloth out.* **CAROL** *sets the plates.*)

CAROL. We only have a few hours left together, and it's Christmas, so let's have something to eat. Okay?

(**CAROL** *goes to the stereo, turns on the Christmas carols, then exits again to the kitchen.* **ALLY** *sits down, looks at* **BO***.*)

ALLY. Bo, c'mon. Just sit down.

(**BO** *doesn't move.*)

This is the last time we're gonna be with her, let's just – . C'mon.

(**CAROL** *re-enters with a large box full of the Costco snack trays. She places a snack tray on each plate.*)

CAROL. It's not much, but it's what we have left.

(**CAROL** *sits down at the table.*)

(*to* **BO**) C'mon, Bo. Christmas dinner.

(**BO** *doesn't sit down.*)

(*silence*)

(*Finally,* **BO** *leaves the room.* **ALLY** *and* **CAROL** *watch him go.*)

ALLY. (*calling out*) Bo. C'mon, just –

(**BO** *re-enters with his bag, shoving clothes into it.*)

Bo, *please* –

BO. I'm not – . I'm not staying here for this.

(*pause*)

I don't know why you need us here, why you need us to watch you – . But I'm not going to.

(**BO** *heads toward the door.*)

CAROL. Bo.

(**BO***, at the door, stops. He doesn't look at* **CAROL***.*)

(*pause*)

You know, I didn't have control over a lot of things in my life. I know your Dad and I weren't perfect, but try growing up with my parents. If I'd have tried to leave when I was seventeen and move to New York City, become a *lesbian...* They'd have shot me dead, I'll tell you that much.

> *(pause)*

I have had very little say in how my life has played out, and I just want this *one last thing*. And I want to have you both here, with me.

> *(pause)*

Please.

> *(silence)*

> *(Then finally, without looking at* **CAROL** *or* **ALLY**, **BO** *exits.)*

> *(The lights snap to black, the television begins to play:)*

Home Video

(CAROL appears on the television.)

CAROL. *(on video)* Alright, well. Your Dad wants me to say something too, but I don't – . Oh, Martin, I don't know, I –

MARTIN. *(on video, offscreen)* It's fine, keep going.

(ALLY sits on the couch, watching the video.)

CAROL. Lately I've been watching his old videos of you two more than he has. The Christmas videos mostly. Fights, lots of fights. Bo being angry. Ally being distant. Tapes are starting to fade. Dad watched them so much, some of them are just completely static.

(pause)

Martin brought this book over the other day that had a picture from this telescope out in space, a picture of all these galaxies, hundreds of them. Nowadays we know exactly where we are, exactly what we are. I think about what my grandparents knew, what their parents knew, their parents and their parents… They must have felt such a responsibility to do things, have kids, move forward, whatever. But now, we know just what and where we are. And it's sort of beautiful, I don't know. Thinking of our place within that – Martin and I, you kids, all these videos of our Christmases fading into static.

(pause)

I hope you kids will watch these, I hope you'll understand what we're doing, I hope – .

(pause, looking away)

Martin I don't want to do this anymore, I don't – Just stop taping me, please just tape over this, I don't want them to –

(The shot cuts out, lights rise on:)

Scene Three

(That evening. ALLY, in funeral black, enters with the potted carnations. She puts the pot down on the floor, then plops down onto the couch.)

(CAROL trails behind ALLY, wearing black denim and a black blouse.)

(CAROL sits down on the couch next to ALLY.)

(pause)

CAROL. It was nice.

ALLY. Fifteen minutes long.

CAROL. Exactly, it was nice. No use in making a big fuss out of anything. The pastor barely knew him anyway.

(pause)

Well, I suppose if Bo didn't go to the funeral, then he probably won't be coming back. Will he?

(pause)

ALLY. I don't – . I'm not sure, Mom.

(pause)

CAROL. But you're staying?

ALLY. Yeah. I'm staying.

(pause)

Mom, why don't – ?

(pause)

I think we should probably – talk.

CAROL. About what?

ALLY. I don't know, just – . We need to like – talk about stuff, right?! This is the last time we're ever going to talk, we need to have big stupid emotional conversations about – stuff!

CAROL. I have no idea what you're saying to me right now.

ALLY. Well you're about to kill yourself, and we barely even talk anymore / and we – !

CAROL. Oh here we go, it's time to have this discussion. Alright, let's get this over with. Number one, we were bad parents.

ALLY. No, that's not what / I mean –

CAROL. Well maybe not *bad* parents, but we could have been better. Two, Dad was filming you all the time. Three, I may have drank too much. And four, after Bo left, we were terrible to you. *But*, you should have brought Max over more. Done! Big issues resolved!

ALLY. *Godammit* why can't we just talk?!

CAROL. Ally, do you think any amount of talking is going to make you feel like we've said everything we needed to say?

(pause)

ALLY. No, probably not.

CAROL. So there we go! Let's just have a pleasant conversation while we still can, alright?

ALLY. Everyone in my life is leaving me, Mom.

(pause)

Laura left me. She took Max. That's why they aren't here.

CAROL. What happened?

ALLY. I – screwed up? I've been working eighty-hour weeks ever since Max was born, I just put down fifty thousand dollars on this bunker on our property without telling her –

CAROL. HOW MUCH MONEY? WHAT'S A BUNKER?

ALLY. Nevermind, it's – . I just messed up, I've been messing things up for a while.

CAROL. Where did she go?

ALLY. Pretty sure she's in Seattle with her cousin.

CAROL. Have you called her?

(pause)

ALLY. Mom, what if I'm not up to this? I've been screwing up the first two years of his life, what's to say I'm not gonna screw up the next sixteen? What if I – ...

CAROL. What? "What if I'm like Dad?" Is that what you were going to say?

(**CAROL** *looks at her, considers for a second.*)

Well, I don't know, maybe you're right. Maybe you shouldn't call them.

(*pause*)

ALLY. Really?

CAROL. Maybe you *would* just screw him up. Maybe you should cut your losses, let them go while he's still young enough to forget about you.

ALLY. Mom –

CAROL. Better yet why don't you just have some of that Nembutal with me? A nice oldfashioned mother-daughter suicide, how about that?

ALLY. OKAY. Okay.

(*pause*)

CAROL. Ally, you – .

(*pause*)

I know what it's like to live in fear of becoming your parents, believe me I get it. So I'm gonna tell you something my parents never told me.

(*pause*)

You're not me. You're not your father. You're thoughtful, driven, and you could be a great parent if you let yourself be. You feel like you spend too much time working? Hire someone. You spent a whole bunch of money on something without telling Laura? Apologize. You're smart enough to fix this.

(*pause*)

ALLY. Yeah.

(pause)

CAROL. So you'll call her?

ALLY. Yeah. I'll call her.

CAROL. Good. That's – good.

(pause)

ALLY. Thank you, Mom.

CAROL. Well, no need to get all sentimental about it.

(Pause. CAROL smiles at her, then gets up.)

Okay, well. You still have the piece of paper, right? The instructions?

(pause)

ALLY. Are we – ? We're doing it now?

CAROL. No reason to wait. You still have the instructions I gave you?

ALLY. Yeah, I – . Yeah.

(pause)

I don't – . I don't know where the Bing Crosby tape is.

CAROL. Oh, don't worry about it.

ALLY. Mom maybe we should wait, maybe Bo will come back –

CAROL. Honey, if he wanted to be here, he'd be here.

(pause)

You sure you want this? I wouldn't blame you for leaving.

ALLY. I want to be here. Really.

(pause)

CAROL. Okay.

(CAROL exits into her bedroom. ALLY sits down on the couch.)

(BO enters, in funeral black. ALLY looks at him.)

ALLY. Hey. You're here.

BO. Yeah.

(pause)

I was on my way to the airport.

ALLY. Why'd you come back?

> *(**CAROL** re-enters with the Nembutal and syringe. She stops when she sees **BO**.)*

CAROL. Well hello.

> *(pause)*

Are you – here?

BO. Mom, were you supposed to do this with Dad? Were you supposed to do this together?

> *(pause)*

CAROL. Bo, why is it so important for / you to – ?

BO. Why do you need us to be here?

> *(pause)*

CAROL. I was going to take it right after he did. Make sure it worked. Then I'd go.

> *(pause)*

ALLY. Why didn't you?

> *(Pause. **CAROL** begins to pace the room, turning on the lights on the Christmas tree, turning on other Christmas decorations, turning on the Christmas carols.)*

CAROL. Dad didn't want you kids involved. But I guess when I saw him sitting there, not breathing, I just – . Still felt like I didn't want to leave.

So I painted everything white, thought maybe that would make me feel better, erasing everything or whatever. But I – realized I wanted you both back here. Every Christmas we always forced you kids to act like you were happy and whatever, and – . I just wanted to have you both here for the holidays one last time. Talk to one another for real. We didn't have many truthful moments with one another, and I thought maybe I could – .

(pause)

CAROL. Thank you, both of you. For being here.

> (**CAROL** *has finished setting up the Christmas decorations, she dims the lights. For the first time the room feels cozy, warm, set up for Christmas.*)

> (**CAROL** *moves to a shelf, picking up a small ceramic vase. She reaches inside of it, pulling out a video tape. She goes to* **BO**, *offering him the tape.*)

It's the last video. The last one we made for you kids. He wanted you to see what it was like, to see that it wasn't scary or sad. I started filming right after he – …

(pause)

Watch it.

> (*Pause.* **BO** *takes the tape. He moves to the television, putting the tape in the camera.*)

> (**CAROL** *moves to the couch, picking up the Nembutal and syringe.*)

> (**BO** *presses play on the camera, the stage transforms into:*)

Last Home Video

(The lights go out, a projection immediately fills the entire space: the old living room, before it was painted white, is projected on top of the present living room. The effect should be that the entire room suddenly returns to what it looked like before it was painted white; for the first time, the room has gained color.)

(An video of **MARTIN** *is projected on the couch;* **CAROL** *and* **MARTIN** *both hold the syringe and Nembutal in their hand. They are rolling up their sleeves, looking for a vein.)*

CAROL. *(on video)* Do you want me to – bring you anything?

MARTIN. *(on video)* Oh it's fine.

CAROL. *(on video)* Do you / want – ?

MARTIN. *(on video)* Honey, it's fine. I'm doing fine. Thanks.

ALLY. How long is to going to take?

CAROL. Not long, I think.

BO. I don't really – . Should we – say something?

CAROL. *(on video)* Should I say something? Read you something?

No.

MARTIN. *(on video)* It's fine.

> *(***CAROL*** and ***MARTIN*** fill their syringes with Nembutal.)*

CAROL. Now I don't want you making a fuss over my funeral. Just keep it simple. Have me cremated.

BO. Okay.

ALLY. You sure it won't hurt?

CAROL. No, not at all. Just drift off to sleep.

MARTIN. *(on video)* I actually feel sort of – optimistic. Like in a few minutes, time and space aren't going to matter. It's almost like I can feel it.

CAROL. *(on video)* Oh you're full of it.

MARTIN. *(on video)* Seriously. You'll feel it too. It's – freeing. In a few days, I'll be cremated, and I'll just be energy spreading out into the universe. Feels pretty good.

> *(**MARTIN** and **CAROL** inject the Nembutal into their arms.)*

CAROL. *(on video)* Martin?

MARTIN. *(on video)* Yeah?

CAROL. *(on video)* Are you going?

BO. You feel okay?

CAROL. Yeah, I feel – good. I feel really good.

MARTIN. *(on video)* I think so.

ALLY. I just wish we knew each other. I wish we all knew each other better.

CAROL. That doesn't matter now.

MARTIN & CAROL. Soon I'll just be energy spreading out into the universe.

> *(pause)*

It really feels sort of – beautiful.

> *(The lights fade out around **BO**, **ALLY**, and the rest of the room; the only light on stage is a small pool of light around **CAROL** and the projection of **MARTIN**.)*

> *(**CAROL** and **MARTIN** breathe in, then out.)*

> *(They breathe in, then out.)*

> *(They breathe in, then out.)*

> *(They breathe in, then are still.)*

> *(a brief moment of silence)*

> *(black)*

End of Play